Lo & Behold

Wendy Mass

Pictures by Gabi Mendez

Colors by Cai Tse

Random House New York

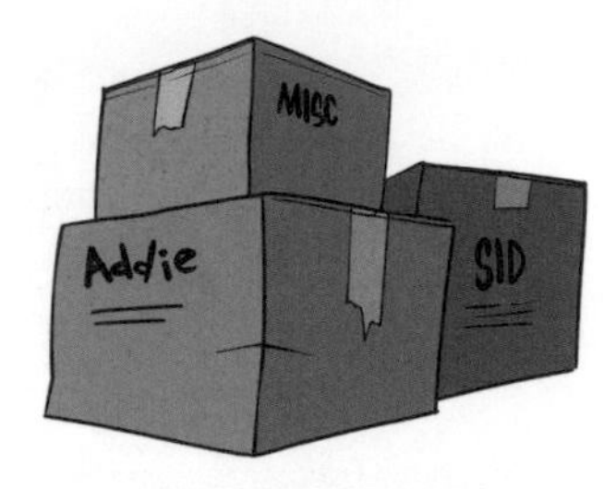

This is a work of fiction. Names, characters, places, and incidents either are the product of the author's imagination or are used fictitiously. Any resemblance to actual persons, living or dead, events, or locales is entirely coincidental.

 Published in the United States by Random House Children's Books, a division of Penguin Random House LLC, New York.

Random House and the colophon are registered trademarks of Penguin Random House LLC.
RH Graphic with the book design is a trademark of Penguin Random House LLC.

Visit us on the Web! rhcbooks.com

Educators and librarians, for a variety of teaching tools, visit us at RHTeachersLibrarians.com

Library of Congress Cataloging-in-Publication Data
Names: Mass, Wendy, author. | Mendez, Gabi, illustrator.
Title: Lo and behold / Wendy Mass; pictures by Gabi Mendez.
Description: First edition. | New York: Random House Children's Books, [2023] | Audience: Ages 8–12. | Summary: "With her life recently turned upside down, 12-year-old Addie is uncomfortable in her own skin until the world of virtual reality sparks her imagination and leads to an exciting new project, a new friend, and to reconnecting with who she's always been"—Provided by publisher.
Identifiers: LCCN 2021043975 | ISBN 978-0-593-17962-8 (paperback) ISBN 978-0-593-17963-5 (hardcover) | ISBN 978-0-593-17964-2 (library binding) ISBN 978-0-593-17965-9 (ebook)
Subjects: CYAC: Graphic novels. | Virtual reality—Fiction. | Friendship—Fiction. | Family life—Fiction. | LCGFT: Graphic novels.
Classification: LCC PZ7.7.M3775 Lo 2023 | DDC 741.5/973—dc23

The artist used Clip Studio to create the illustrations for this book.
The text of this book is set in 10-point Tucker Script.
Interior design by April Ward

MANUFACTURED IN CHINA
10 9 8 7 6 5 4 3 2 1
First Edition

For Mike, who always encourages me
to pursue whatever lights me up and
never complains when I bring home
yet another VR headset.

—W.M.

To all my people I can't see
every day, I'm so grateful we can love
and support each other even if
I can't hold your hands.

—G.M.

Hey, readers . . . head over to
wendymass.com/Lo-and-Behold
to find out how you can add some
augmented reality to this book!

Virtual reality connects humans to other humans in a profound way. . . . Through this machine, we become more compassionate, we become more empathetic, and we become more connected. And ultimately, we become more human.

—Chris Milk, VR creator

Only when it is dark enough can you see the stars.

—Martin Luther King Jr.

"The best time to plant a tree was twenty years ago.
The second best time is NOW.

Prologue

The tree didn't look like much back then.
The first time Mom let me dress myself.

I won it by being the only kindergartner able to identify five Skittles flavors while blindfolded.
Green apple!

THIS AWARD IS PRESENTED TO
ADDIE
FOR
BEING BEST CANDY GUESSER

This may be the only time I'm glad you inherited my sweet tooth.

CONGRATS
ADDIE BRECKER
first hat trick in PeeWee Soccer
DIPLOMA
TO
ADDIE BRECKER
FOR
Learning her ABC's

Honk honk
We weren't supposed to plant anything behind our apartment. But Dad had a plan.

My parents are big on traditions, so we started a new one.
Our growing tree
AGE 6¾

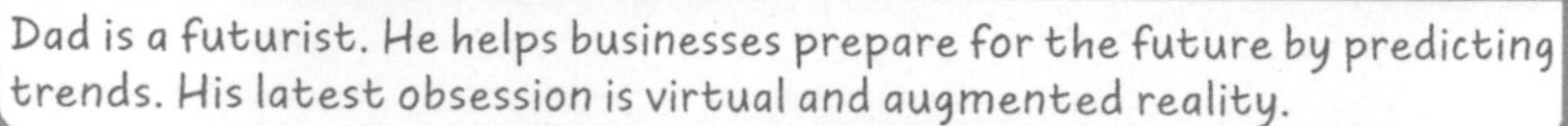
Dad is a futurist. He helps businesses prepare for the future by predicting trends. His latest obsession is virtual and augmented reality.

AGE 7¾

AGE 8¾
Mom used to give tours at the zoo. She and Dad first met in front of the giant tortoise enclosure. She got really into tortoises after that.

AGE
9 3/4

When I was ten, Mom fell off her bike avoiding a bunny and had to have major surgery.
AGE ⇨
10 3/4
Things went downhill slowly.
AGE
11 3/4
This was the last time we took a family picture.

I'm trying, Dr. Maron, but she won't listen.

500 MG
2
TAKE 2 TABL
FOR PAIN

And then really fast.

For all Dad's future-predicting skills, he neglected to predict *this*.

The neighbors felt sorry for me.
Whisper whisper

Dad tried to lift my mood.

nal Rescue
PUPPY DAY!!
Adoption
9:30-5:30
Want to visit the puppies?

I didn't want to see anything trapped.

It's been a year now, and I'm getting used to the new normal. But I still don't feel quite right in my skin.

Chapter One

LOVE YOU
THE MOON
AND BACK
Knock knock
Addie? Are you finished packing?
The Tale of a Tortoise
Almost, Dad!
I NEED SPACE
Did you say goodbye to your friends yet?
I actually said goodbye to them a year ago. It wasn't anybody's fault. We didn't know what to say to each other anymore.

Our trip should really be called Dad Drags Addie a Thousand Miles Away for His Summer Job Whether She Wants to Go or Not, but that's not as snappy.

Dad's job as a futurist is actually not as boring as it sounds.

Or ridden in the back of a self-driving car. It was awesome, but Mom was nauseous for two days.
Woo-hoo!
Dad promises this gig won't be boring, either. He says there will be ivy-covered buildings, maybe even a moat. (I think he was kidding about the moat.) But it's far away from home and that feels weird.
And don't fill your suitcase with turtles!
Tortoises!
I know. I just like to annoy you.
When you're named after the world's longest-living tortoise, you get a lot of tortoise stuff.

I know Shelly's not the most original name for a tortoise, but I named her when I was two. Full name: Shellyface Tortybutt.

Shelly's twin, Lightning, used to sleep here. Mom sewed a lightning bolt onto his forehead so we could tell them apart. He went missing a year ago.

The tortoise I'm named after was called Adwaitya. He didn't go into space, but he had a lot of adventures in his 250 years on Earth.

As much as Mom loved tortoises, her first love was outer space. Mine, too.

She couldn't be an astronaut because of the motion-sickness issue. But I used to dream of going to the moon.

But that was just a dumb dream. The moon missions are over. I won't get my chance.

Addie! You've got to see this! It's not a virtual reality thing, I promise.

Dad's knowledge of VR is the reason he landed this job. He can make me go with him, but he can't make me interested.
GADGETS
GIZMOS
There are a lot of boxes. We're still only going for the summer, right? Because I promised Shelly.
Maybe not the best idea to admit I'm talking to a stuffed animal.
Look!

SPRING HAVEN UNIVERSITY
Chosen to plant MOON TREE
for Bicentennial celebration
August 27, 1976
Good try, Dad. That article almost looks real.
I NEED SPACE

It is real. This is the school's official website. And you love those moon seeds.

Eh, they're okay.

HAHAHAHAHA
We both know I'm obsessed with the moon seeds. I got an A+ on my project in fifth grade.

FROM MOON SEEDS...
A+
Could ordinary seeds go into space, survive without Earth's gravity, and still turn into trees? Let's find out!
REDWOOD SEEDS
LOBLOLLY PINE
SYCAMORE SEEDS
The forestry service needed to find the right astronaut. They found him in this brave man who loved trees so much he jumped into flames to save them!
STUART ROOSA
SMOKEJUMPER
DATE: 1971
WHOOSH!
RUMBLE
Alan Shepard and Edgar Mitchell went to the surface to conduct experiments...
...and have a little fun!

Roosa and the seeds circled the moon thirty-four times before coming back to pick up his friends two days later.
"It took a cast of thousands to get us up and back!"
But when the seeds got to the lab they blew up!
But most of the five hundred seeds still germinated! How amazing is that?
I hope I get to visit one someday!
In 1976 the trees were planted all across the world, connecting the Earth and the moon.
...TO MOON TREES!
by Addie Brecker

Hmm. The article doesn't say if the sapling was ever actually planted, but a lot of trees weren't recorded.
tap-tap
print

Knew it was too good to be true.
I NEED SPACE

ADDIE'S TOWEL
SID'S TOWE

CONGRATS
Addie Brecker
First Pee-Wee Soccer Hat Trick

When Mom was little she used to wish on stars.
But we can't see any here because of all the city lights, so there's nothing to wish on. Sometimes I can spot the moon, though.

This was the first of many pillows Mom made after her accident to help distract her from the pain.
LOVE YOU TO THE MOON AND BACK

XO
MOMMY

Chapter Two

ROAD TRIP:
DAY 1
It's uncivilized to be awake this early.

AM FM XM
6 60's on 6
7 Symphony
8 Stuck in the
9 XM Cafe
Channel
9:24
A/C

"But girls they wanna have fun, oh girls just wanna have . . ."

TAP
TAP
TAP

"Oh daddy dear you know you're still number one, but girls they wanna have fun."

You don't have to hide when you're happy, you know.

I know.
I love my dad, but the truth is I still kind of blame him for not being able to help Mom more.

I think he knows it, too.

But actually . . .
Mom! how could you miss t parent teacher conference?
That was today?
I told you three times!! it was so embarrassing...
... I'm sorry

I also blame me.

Quality MOTEL
He kind of looks like me, huh?

BZZZ
BZZZZ

Yes, this is he. Is everything okay?

Yes, of course. We'll only be away for six weeks.

The next morning

!
I think these are supposed to look like us!
They kind of do!

Dad's more of an "order takeout" kind of guy (when he remembers meals at all), so ya gotta eat as much as you can when you can.

See anywhere fun to stop? Your choice.

WORLD'S LARGEST BALL OF TWINE

Hmm. Maybe?
Dinosaur Land
Amazing! REALISTIC!

Kinda cool . . .
CAVERN INFORMATION

Dad!!
TURN HERE
nation's third largest impact crater

Woo-hoo!
squeal!
TURN HERE

A piece of outer space landed right here!

SPRINGHAVE
IF YOU CAN'T

I don't see any ivy. Or a moat.
Just wait. You will.

Home away from home.

Faculty Housing est. 1963

Hey, Mr. Brecker! Welcome to S.H.U.!

Shay! Hello! Do you live in this building, too?
No, sir. I'm buds with the family across the hall from you.

Let me help with those.

Shay's one of my students. Wait till you see what he's working on. Mind-blowing stuff!
And he's cute, am I right?

Dad! Ew, gross!
He's totally cute.

Looks like other kids live here. Could be new friends.

Please just try.

Shay and I will finish lugging everything. You go unpack your room.

Doesn't feel like home away from home.

At least I'm not the only artist to have lived in this room.

page 2

Plunk
Done.

Yuck,
gross!

You might
want to hold
your nose.

I guess
we're ordering
in tonight.

Nope. This is a
summer of trying
new things.
We're going
to the market,
and I'm cooking!

What's that smell?

That's fresh country air. Breathe it in.

Wow. That's more exercise than I've seen Dad do in a lifetime.

Impressive!
Haven't played since college. Guess I still got it.

Okay, mostly got it.

Shay's working on a virtual reality exercise game. I'll try it if you will.
SPRING HAVEN SUPER

Not sure. Remember the first—and last—time you put a VR headset on Mom?
I regret mentioning Mom as soon as it's out of my mouth.

In hindsight, it probably wasn't a good idea to start her off on a virtual roller coaster.

The last time Dad cooked he almost burned the apartment down.

No shame in turning back now. That Thai menu looked really good.

This market shall not defeat me!

Dad! Pretty sure that's not how you do it!

When Mom was a teenager she once wheeled a whole cart full of candy out the door and got grounded for a year.

WOW
BRIGHT DAY
Natural & Organic
JUST D
GOO

OH YEAH
SNICKERDOODLE
CHOCOLATE CHIP
Funky Fresh

But it's not stealing if someone's still going to pay for it.
WATERMELON 3

He shoots, he scores!

TSK
TSK

Just keep on walking. The last thing I need is some kid teasing me right now.

Excuse me.
Busted.

Are you Sid Brecker? I'm Paula Vargas.
Or not!

Addie, this is Professor Vargas, our new neighbor. She connected me with Shay and the other students I'll be working with.

Shay's been in our family's lives for a long time.
Plus, your dad's famous in the biz.

Nice to meet you.
My son Mateo is about your age. I'm hoping you two will become great friends.

Blue hair dye? Not sure this is how great friendships start.
Shhh . . .
HAIR DYE

Don't try this at home.
You make a confusing first impression.
Hey, how'd this get in here?
?

That night

LOVE YOU TO
THE MOON

I know this one's your favorite.
LOVE YOU TO THE MOON AND BACK
Used to be my favorite.

Hey, thanks for bringing this stuff. And for letting me keep the snacks.

I figure you can share it with your new buddy.
Let's not get ahead of ourselves.

Good night, honey. We'll get our school ID cards in the morning and then we'll really feel like we belong.

I doubt an ID card can do that.
LOVE YOU TO
THE MOON
XO
MOMMY

Chapter Three

Excuse me, were you working here in 1976?
Do I look old enough to have been working here in 1976?

Um . . .
The answer is no, of course you don't.
What my daughter means is, do you know if a moon tree was ever planted on campus?

Don't know what that is. But North Campus had a fire in the '80s.
If a tree was planted in the Grove, it would have burned with the rest.

But on the bright side, here's a Spring Haven University pencil for each of you!

I'll keep asking around about the tree. But at least we're officially members of campus now. Isn't that exciting?
I think we have different definitions of exciting. Couldn't this school have found a better mascot? No one likes bees.

Hey, if all the honeybees died out, all the crops they pollinate would go extinct, and we kinda need those.

I know, Dad.
I also know if the rain forest was destroyed, the extra carbon would poison the planet, and after a nuclear war, roaches and scorpions would rule the world.

So you *do* hear me when I talk after all. But until any of that stuff happens, you're free to roam the campus while I'm at work.

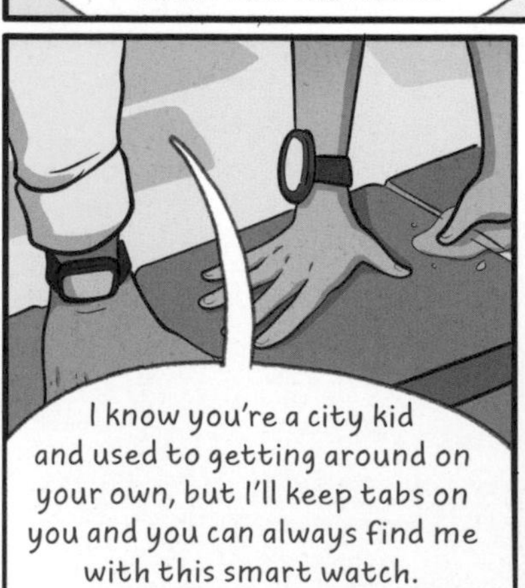
I know you're a city kid and used to getting around on your own, but I'll keep tabs on you and you can always find me with this smart watch.

Or I can just wait at the apartment?

You're going to need to find some things to do. I'll leave you with a campus map. Or should I ask Professor Vargas what Mateo is up to?
No.

These will keep you busy.

Your augmented reality glasses? Don't you need them to catch Pokémon?
Very funny. You know I've caught 'em all.

One of my students, Lily, is working on a grant to set up augmented reality public art.
Wait till you see her portals!

I know better than to ask what an augmented reality portal is or he'll actually tell me.

See, told you there was ivy and a moat.
WOW!

I can't *wait* for you to see what else these students are working on, Addie. They're going to change the world.

That's a nice thought, but I'm not even sure people can change themselves, let alone the whole world.

I told you, Chaz and I are just friends!
Sure you are! Then why were you sharing nachos at the campus center last night?

Seriously, Tommy? Friends can't share nachos?

I know
martial arts.
I don't know martial arts.

So you're stalking me now?
You're in *my* reading spot.

Prove it.

That could just be a coincidence.
MATEO'S SPOT

Hey!
Too slow. Like the tortoise and the hare. You're the tortoise in this scenario, in case you were wondering.
Trust me, I'm always the tortoise.

Cool boots. You're not hot in them?
Nope.
Maybe a little.

They used to be my mom's. She's not . . . she's not using them right now.

Mateo's not asking about Mom. That must mean Dad told Professor Vargas what happened, and she told Mateo. Fine. Makes things easier.

If you must know, it's a story about a real giant tortoise named Adwaitya who lived for two hundred and fifty years.

My parents named me after him for good luck or something. It's moving kind of . . . slowly, though.

Then his life's probably not that exciting.

Actually, it is! First, he was snatched from his island and sent far away to live with strangers.

But they took good care of him. He got to meet famous people from history!

And when he was—

Hold on. I know this really happened and all, but when does the plucky sidekick come in?

Sigh.
Never mind. Let's talk about something else.

How long have you lived here?
All my life. My dad works at the hospital. We live on campus because of my mom.

Then you'd know if there was a moon tree on campus?

Moon tree? Are you just putting random words together? Like hand house. Or dust bunny?

A dust bunny is a real thing. So are moon trees. They grew from seeds that traveled around the moon on Apollo 14.
These seeds never actually *landed* on the moon?
So what's the big deal? No offense.

Soon there won't be any human beings alive who made it to the moon.
But these trees will remind us of our achievements.

Is this for school or something?

Sigh

Well, I have a project.
PAY IT FORWARD
Must be easy to pay it forward when your life is easy.
C'mon, you can help me with it.
It's not like I have anything better to do.
That's the spirit!
How'd you pick my tree, anyway?
I was on that bench, but then those college kids started arguing. I think they're breaking up.
Guess they made up.
College kids are weird. Shay has a new girlfriend each week.
It's cool to have someone my own age to hang around with.
Yeah, well, don't get used to it.
SpringHaven Library
I'll grow on you—you'll see.

My dad says that the best way to do a good deed is anonymously. The second best is any other way.

That reminds me of something my mom once sewed on a pillow.

"Addie's at the library"
Buzz buzz
What's that?

That's my dad checking on me. Here, you can play with these.

Happy to see you're exploring campus.

When did all this *stuff* get here? Is that a . . . *dragon*?

Mateo dragged me along. What's up?
My students are ready for beta testers. Mateo, we could use you, too.

No, thank you . . . I've got to, um, clean my room.
Suit yourself. I'm on my way to get you, Addie!

These glasses are awesome, thank you!
You have to clean your room, huh?

I've learned my lesson about volunteering on campus after helping my mom do a unit on global warming.
She made me hold an ice pop while the class recorded how long it took to melt under different conditions.

You poor thing. Sounds terrible.

Hey, I held eight ice pops and didn't get to eat any of them!
Hope you have better luck!

I found food trucks, Addie! Isn't college life grand?

They're no ice pops, but at least they won't melt!

And then he didn't even wait to see if someone found the dollar!
Sounds like a thoughtful boy.
This is where you work?
When the university says you can have space for free, you grab it.
I can see why it's free.

Um, Dad?
LEAVE WHENCE YOU CAME

Don't worry. The Gang has a strange sense of humor.
BEWARE TURN BACK NOW
STAY OUT

Bzzz
snap
Here we are!
ATTACK OF THE KILLER SQUID

What, no retinal scan? A secret password at least?
I'll have to suggest that.

Hang in There
Don't forget to be

SID!!!!!
IN VR

Hehe. They love doing that.
Dad clearly loves it, too.
Hi, Gang! This is my daughter, Addie.
Hi, um . . . Gang?
ADDIE!
Me, not so much.
Isn't it amazing? Let me show you around.
This is Doug. He's working on an app that will revolutionize social VR. Plus, if you ever need a computer built overnight from scratch, he's your guy.
I plan to never need that.

Are the magnets part of your VR project?
Nope.
I was struck by lightning when I was ten, and now I can magnetize things by rubbing my hands together. I just do it when I need a break from coding.

Um . . . cool?

Let's check out what Lily's doing. She made the augmented reality art you saw outside.

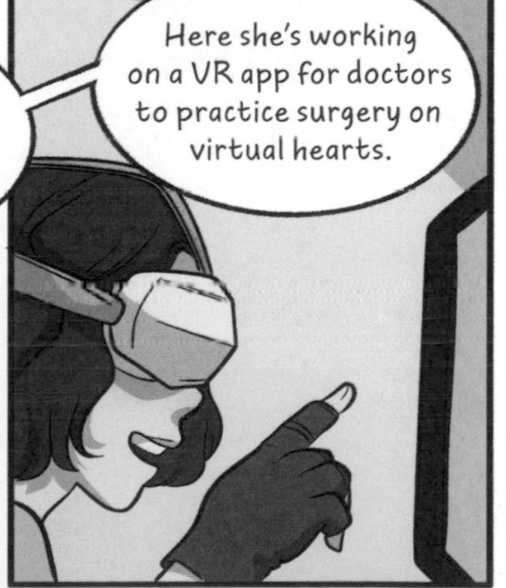
Here she's working on a VR app for doctors to practice surgery on virtual hearts.

Isn't it great? I can even make it beat!

Hi, Addie! I'm Surekha! Your dad said you haven't tried much VR before. I can't wait to show you the coolest things— we are going to be *such* good friends.
Did you know it took humans 125,000 generations to get from the caves to the industrial revolution? And then only *ten* generations to where we are now?
With VR, we create our own worlds and literally step inside them! Imagine what opportunities *your* kids will have!
My . . . kids?
Surekha is what we call a *VR evangelist*. That's someone who wants to put everyone in the world in a headset.
I think her project on cultivating empathy is especially important.

Ready?

?

Hey, everyone, I may have overloaded the circuits with the VR bike so don't be surprised if—

Pop! Hisssss
—the power goes out.

I know an opportunity when I see one.
Bye, Dad! See ya at dinner.

Blah blah so exciting blah cutting edge blah blah nothing like it before. Blah blah blah.

Blah blah doing so much good blah blah grant proposals due in a few weeks blah blah can't wait to try more blah blah.

Blah blah love you, honey, blah blah great dinner blah blah.

Nice dining with you, Dad.

Chapter Four

BAM BAM
POW

Nice ducks.
Oh, hey!

You were cute when you were little.
That's . . . my brother, Emilio.

Let me guess. You were Woody that year.
No. I've never seen Toy Story.

Can you do anything with this to make it look less like a five-year-old made it? It's supposed to inspire my summer class.

LASTIC CUPS
4 PLASTIC BOTTLES
FOUND INSIDE THIS BEACHED WHALE
25 PLASTIC BAGS
2 FLIP-FLOPS
UHHH...

Emilio must have helped make it. I don't want to insult him.
100 PLASTIC CUPS

I think it's perfect as it is. Makes you want to hug the whale.
And, you know, never wear flip-flops again. Or use plastic.

Welcome to life with an environmentalist. Mom just finished teaching a unit on pesticides and genetically modified food. All we ate last month was air.
He exaggerates. We also had water.

Counters are for food, Mateo.

Mom, don't!

That's a lot of maps.
Going on a road trip?

No.

Maps?
Are you taking
her geocaching?

Yes! Geocaching!
Let's go! Bye,
Mom!

Feel like telling
me what that
was about?
Nope.

To the woods! We're going to use the GPS on my phone to find hidden treasures called caches. You'll love it.

Here, we'll start with the best one on campus.
Mateo's Myst
W
45
FEET
S
E
Something tells me I know who hid it.
As we get closer to the cache, the compass will count down, then we'll use our geo-senses to find it.
Hey, city girl! Didn't anyone ever teach you not to stick your arm down a hole without looking?
Want a hint?
Nope.

Lo and behold! I found it!
Very good for a first-timer.

You just *assumed* I was a first-timer. My parents and I went geocaching all the time.
LOG

BUS STOP
TARGET FOUND
We went a little more high-tech, though.

Why didn't you stop me?
And miss all that good mansplaining?
Very funny.

Found your cache with
son before leaving him here
his first day of college. Thank you
a special memory
Signed, Weepymom2
GEOCACHING GOT THIS 85-YEAR-
OLD OFF THE COUCH AND BACK INTO
THE WORLD. WEARING YOUR MONSTER
FINGER NOW
SIGNED, GEOGRANDPA

If you copied these comments into your school notebook, you'd definitely get an A for making these people so happy!

First cache with Mateo.
Had a good teacher.
Signed, Tortybutt

Your geocaching name is Tortybutt?

It's actually Tortybutt-in-Space. I used to want to be an astronaut and go to the moon.

That's cool. Couldn't you still be one?
I don't know. It feels complicated.

I have no idea what I want to be. But I do know that the food truck outside the math building has the best churros outside Argentina.
After a long hike, it's important to stay hydrated, you know.

This was a hike? Plus, I don't think churros are hydrating.

They are when you suck out the dulce de leche and use them as a straw to drink chocolate milk!

Okay, he might be growing on me after all.

So what do you usually do all day in the summer?
Just chill, mainly. Sometimes I volunteer to help some of the older patients at the hospital.
You should come. It's right down the next street.

Yeah, maybe.

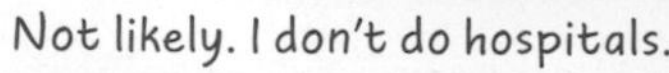
Not likely. I don't do hospitals.

Rumor around campus is that building's haunted.

People have seen ghosts in the basement window!
Those aren't ghosts! Those are my dad's students doing their virtual reality projects.

Virtual reality? That's Shay's big secret project? I have to see this!
Didn't your mom tell you about my dad's job?

Do *you* listen when parents talk about other grown-ups?
Good point.
And don't worry about all those warnings. . . . They are just—okay, guess you're not worried.
GIANT CAT
MARS
ATTACK
SPACE
EVIL SCIENCE
You brought your friend! How wonderf—
Dad!
Mine!

The others have tried my empathy project so they can't be impartial. Need new blood. Not literally, of course.
I'm your guy. Put me in a headset!
Man, gets me every time.
Matty boy!
So this is where you've been hiding out.
Sorry I couldn't tell you what I was working on. All very hush-hush till beta. Glad you're here!
Mateo's in good hands with Surekha.
Would you like to try my exercise game? I'd love your opinion.

I better stay here to make sure Mateo doesn't cause any trouble.
Smart.
I can still hear you, you know.
No roller coaster, right?
Yes! I love roller coasters!
Roller coasters will have to wait.
11:19 AM
EMPATHY PROJECT
360 Dog Simulation
START
CODE NAME: JASPER
When is it going to—ooh!

It's like I'm RIGHT THERE!

Hey, puppy. Aren't you so cute? Good doggies!
Giggle

Hey . . . oh no . . .

This has taken an odd turn.
But . . . but . . .

Oh!! Oh! Awwww. Phew.

Are you okay?
It just felt so real. That dog, Jasper . . .
Did it make you want to take Jasper home?
Surekha, we talked about this.
You can't go after your test subjects to adopt the dogs.

That was intense. You should try it.
I try to avoid crying on command.

How about we go shoot zombies out of fire hoses?
You mean go shoot zombies *with* fire hoses?
Nope.

Addie, if you don't want to try it, at least let Surekha tell you about her project.
That's dad-speak for *you're staying here.*

Sooo . . . empathy?

Glad you asked. In 2015, the *New York Times* sent out 1.3 million Google Cardboard VR headsets with a 360-degree video that followed three young war refugees. It was an experiment in cultivating empathy. That's what inspired my work.

Empathy is different from sympathy. A person *expresses sympathy* to provide comfort.

But they *share empathy* when they are able to feel what the other feels.

For empathy you need to:

1. See from the other person's perspective.
2. Suspend judgment. JUDGMENT
3. Be able to tap into your own feelings.
4. Communicate honestly so the other person feels heard and understood.

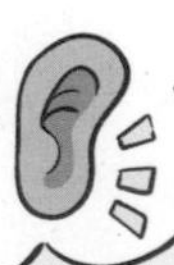

We work hard at avoiding pain, so taking on someone else's requires strength.

It takes practice. My goal is to jump-start a person's ability to empathize by literally letting them walk in another's shoes.

I have much more to my project than Mateo saw. You could do a different part?
Caught you, you evil but oddly cute skeleton creature! Huzzah!
...

Lost another one to Shay. Just go.
Sorry!
Sigh

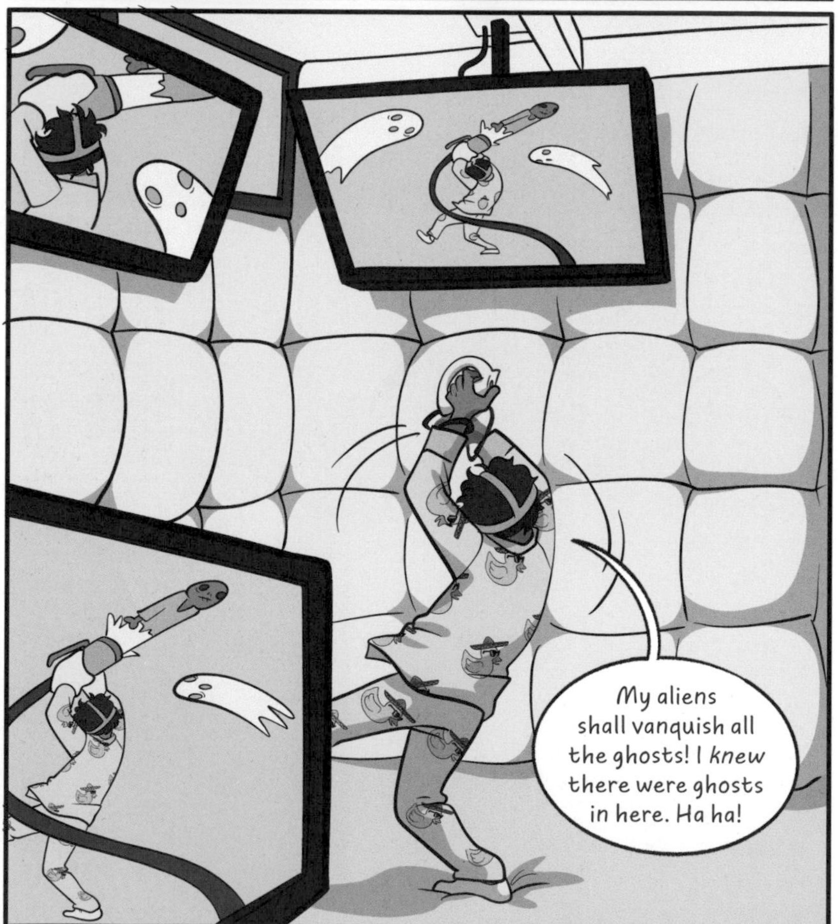
My aliens shall vanquish all the ghosts! I *knew* there were ghosts in here. Ha ha!

That's the goal. Making people sweat one monster at a time. If they're having fun, they don't realize they're exercising.

Ready to be transported to another world?
Mateo already signed you in.

For someone who spent the last year wishing she was someplace else, why are my hands sweating?

Pull yourself together. This is supposed to be fun.

Okay, I'm ready.

There are only two buttons and a trigger.
If you get too close to the walls, a green boundary line will pop up. Try not to ignore those, like your friend here.
Got it. Won't ignore boundaries like the kid I just met two days ago.
Heard that.

Remember, I'll be able to see what you see, so if you need any help, just ask.

Ready to battle some ghosts?
As I'll ever be.

Just blackness. I don't think it works for me.

Wait. What was that?

Are you KIDDING ME?!

Chapter Five

I'm like . . . inside a video game! A beautiful one!

I wonder if they know I'm here. Wait, they're not real.

Mmm . . . I swear I can smell the apples. I must have a better imagination than I thought!

HAHA! I didn't think that would work! But can I eat it?
SLICE

Chomp Chomp
Ha!

Huh? Now I have foam fingers?
Whoa!
Hahaha!
Whoosh
Shwwwoooo
Take *that*, you creepy ghosts with the sad eyes that make me want to like you.
Whoosh
Ahhh
Splat!
Ding ding ding
CONGRATULATIONS, TORTYBUTT!! YOU ARE AT THE TOP OF THE LEADERBOARD!!
Also, Mateo's gonna pay for putting that name in.
Woo-hoo!

LEVEL 2
VEGETABLES
Vegetables?
I need those swords back!
Fwoop
Fwoop
Hey, I can teleport!! Watch out, broccoli. I'm coming for you!
I can feel the wind in my hair!
I am *killing* this!
LEVEL 3
fwoop
crackle
boom
Aw!

Whoa, I'm still in the basement! That's so weird!
Twenty minutes? It felt like five!
That's a common reaction. So how'd you like it?
It was *amazing*.
So much better than I'd expected. Thank you.
Thank *you*! And you have some admirers.
Clap. clap
Woo-hoo
Yay for Tortybutt!
I couldn't get past Level Two! You didn't mention how good you were at video games.
I didn't know!

Q1. How would you rate your VR experience today,
on a scale from 1 to 10, where 1 is *Total Snore, I'd*
have been getting a cavity filled, to 10, *Best thing in*
the universe.
A1: I rate it a 9.9. If it was in outer space, it would have
been a 10. It was funny and fun and beautiful. I
changed my mind . . . 10!
you feel like you got a full-body workout? Why
hurt that I didn't know I had.
suggestions for improvement?
the castle.

Come see! I'm riding my bike in China!!
That's so cool! Can you go anywhere?

Mateo?

Sorry. I'm not sure. But maybe?

It's wonderful to see you so excited about something.

How do I explain to him what it felt like to be somewhere else? The freedom to be some*one* else?

Are you ready to try Surekha's empathy project?

And let Mateo beat my high score on Shay's game? No chance. When can I play it again?

I have a headset you can use in the bottom drawer of the desk in the living room. It has the Gang's projects on it.

Gotta go! See you later!

What's the rush? Craving a churro as much as I am?

Yup, you caught me.

If I tell him about Dad's headset, he'll want to use it, and I don't want to share yet.

Did you notice the apples really smelled like apples? And the wind was blowing?
You mean the apples from the bowl on Shay's desk and the wind from the fan?
I'm sorry. Should I not have told you?
That's okay. I know VR isn't magic.
But it sure felt like it.

You must be Addie. Would you like to join us for lunch? I'd give my empanadas a B minus.

Trust me, anything is better than last month when all we ate was air!

And water, right?
Haha, yes, and water.

Thanks for the offer, but a grilled cheese sandwich is calling my name.
And a VR headset!

I like her. She's feisty.

Yeah, you definitely don't want to attack her castle.

Ten minutes later
It tastes better than it looks.
And away we go.

Shay:
VR for Fitness
Lily:
VR for Training
Immersion Therapy
Surekha:
Empathy Project
Doug:
Social VR
Greetings, Mr. Brecker! We hope you love our demos. Start anywhere.
Shay:
VR for Fitness
Sign In!
TORTYBUTT
FINISH
1 2 3 4 5 6 7 8 9 0
Q W E R T Y U I O P
A S D F G H J K L
Z X C V B N M , .
I'm back! And pretty sure I still smell apples.

Whoosh
Shwump
Thwap
Woo-hoo!
LEVEL 4

HEADSET POWER IS VERY LOW
RECHARGE NOW
SO YOU DON'T LOSE PROGRESS
Noooooo...

GIZMOS
Aplenty

portable battery

That'll do it.

"He's the boogie woogie bugle boy of Company B. A toot, a toot, a toot diddleyada toot."
Guess they like old-timey music over there.

GO TO THE ROOF
DRESS APPROPRIATELY

How do I dress appropriately? Oh, I'm in a raincoat! Now how do I get up there?

Tell me your secrets, wall.

Oh! Neat!

Haha! This is awesome.

And exhausting! Pretty sure the castle is getting taller!

meow
meow
Aw, cute!
HERD ALL THE CATS INTO THE CAT CONDO ON THE ROOF.

!!

Heeeeyyyyy! Not cool!

GAME OVER. THANK YOU FOR PLAYING THIS DEMO.
I HOPE YOU LIKED IT.
Rats.
Purr purrrr

I wonder what immersion therapy is. . . .
Shay:
VR for Fitness
Lily:
VR for Training
Immersion Therapy
Surekha:
Empathy Project
Doug:
Social VR
THIS SHORT DEMO WILL LET YOU FACE YOUR FEAR OF HEIGHTS!
Holy smokes, Batman!! Okay, so *this* is immersion therapy!
CONQUER YOUR FEAR OF SPIDERS!
Oh, heck no! Next!

Ahhh, that heart again!
Anything but that.

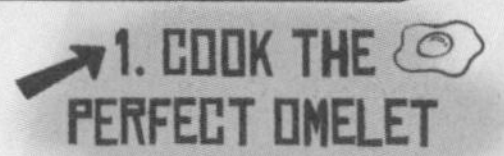

2. LEARN TO SALSA

4. PERFORM OPEN HEART SURGERY

Hi! I'm heading to the hospital for my volunteer gig now. Ready to come with?
Uh, can't. Have an errand to do.

Do you, um, want to come in?

That's okay. Good luck with your errand.

Chapter Six

Hello? Anyone here?
Just me. Everyone's in a meeting off campus.
Could actually use a little help.

Remind me not to dance in VR without unplugging the cords first!

Thanks. Owe you one.

This died, and there's no way to charge it.
Did you switch out the battery?

Good as new. Have you tried my Social VR app yet?
What does it do again?
You can meet up with your friends or other people from around the world to play games, travel, watch movies,
LITTLEGREYFRIEND
CATKNIGHT23
take classes, go to concerts and sporting events, you name it.
My demo has computer-generated NPCs—non-player characters—so you can practice by talking to them.
Remember, the same rules apply in social VR as when talking to strangers on the internet—don't exchange personal information, watch out for trolls, you know the drill.

Thanks, I'll check it out.

I probably won't, though. Talking to real people is hard enough.

Thanks For Playing!
Ah, poop. No more Lily.

Surekha:
Empathy Project

Doug:
Social VR

Fine, Doug. Let's meet these NPCs of yours.
Social VR

BUILD YOUR AVATAR!

Neat! But looks too much like me.

DEFAULT
ACCEPT AVATAR

ACCEPT AVATAR

Better.

ENTER MAIN LOBBY

ROCKET LAUNCH
MOVIE TIME
Rocket launch??

Ten seconds to liftoff. Ten... nine... eight...
ROAR
whoosh
Seven... six... five... four...
Three... two... one! Liftoff!
Ooooohhhhh!
!!

Oh—how wonderful! It's so real! I feel like I'm in a dream.

I know, right? But in my dreams I'm always late for a test in a class I never went to.

Are you talking to me?
Weren't you talking to me first?

But you're not real . . . right?

Real as it gets. Let me guess, first-timer?

Not cool, Doug! You said these were computer-generated people!

I'm not Doug . . . My name's—

knock
knock

Oh.
Hi, Dad.

You've been having fun with that, I take it?

I saw a *real-live* rocket launch! I also made a virtual omelet!
Well, half an omelet.
That's fantastic!

I'm sorry to dash in and out, but I'm afraid it will be a week of late nights at the lab.

You have a standing invitation for dinner across the hall.
I'm sure Mateo is eager to have someone to hang out with.

Actually, I'm planning to cook a *real* omelet for dinner.
Mateo has his little brother, Emilio, for company.

I didn't know he had a brother. But still, it's not the same as a peer. You can show Mateo the demos.

I guess you saw the letters. I brought them for when you're ready.

You'll be okay alone, then?
Yup.

Twenty minutes later
I may need more training.

Midnight . . .

Hi, honey, sorry if I woke you. This is delicious.
?

The next morning
Thanks For Playing
Thanks For Playing
I was hoping they'd have reset overnight.

Maybe that guy who spoke to me was an NPC after all and I overreacted. Or Doug tricked me so I'd be more social. Guess I should find out.
Social VR

BUILD YOUR AVATAR!

Hmm, maybe.
Nah. Not a feather boa type of robot.

That's the one!

WELCOME BACK TO MAIN LOBBY

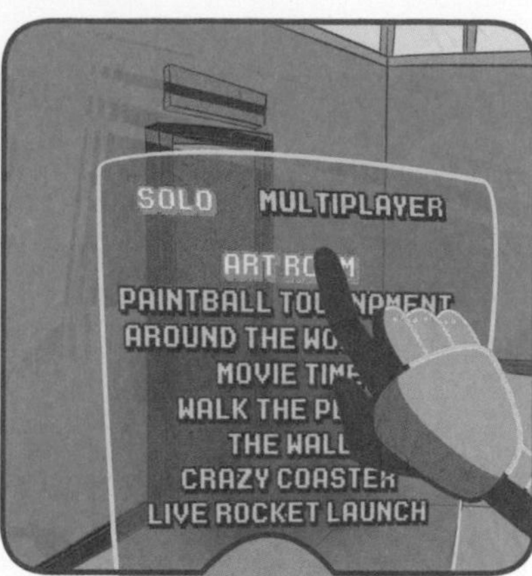

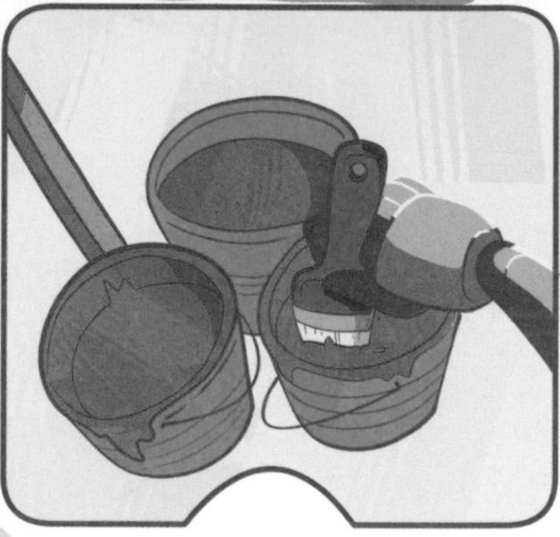

Ohhh, that's coooool. I'm painting in the air!

Knock
Knock
Knock
Knock

I can hear you breathing. Wanna go for a bike ride into town? The candy factory sometimes gives out free samples.

I'm kind of in the middle of working on something.

Your book? Will I get to see it sometime?
Um, sure.

Okay, bye! Have fun.

Oh no, my sculpture must not have saved.

Was I supposed to press that? Maybe if I press this it will come back.

Whoa! Okay, not the right button.
But totally awesome!!
Buzz buzz
Want to grab lunch with the Gang?
I'm inside a painting of a boat!
ART DEMO ENDING IN
3...
2...
1...
Aw!

MAIN LOBBY
ART ROOM

NPCs or not, I suddenly feel like I'm the new kid in school.

!

Hi again, hope I didn't scare you off the other day.
Um . . . no offense, but I'm still not sure if you're real.

You're right. She *is* funny.

She has a point, though. What's real, and what's an illusion?
Maybe the universe is made of math and each person is only a representation of a mathematical equation.

Or maybe it's only when we're dreaming that we're truly awake, or—

If you don't talk about math anymore, I won't doubt your realness again.
Okay. But you're missing out on my best theories that time is an illusion.

Nice bees.
Nice turtles.
They're tortoises.

How'd you know that?
Figure with a VR avatar named Tortybutt, they'd have to be tortoises.

How'd you know my VR name?
Tortybutt
It pops up when I point over your head.
RunsWithWings
JustJane, huh?
What you see is what you get with me.
JustJane
PB in five!
Paintball's starting! Let's go!
I don't know. I've never—
—played before.

Chapter Seven

Torty! We've gotta go. They always check here first.

Fwoop
Splat
Ahhhh
Gahhh
You're fast!
I can't run in real life so I got good at it in VR.

Addie?

Look out behind you! It's Jane and SmolPotat!

Huh? Who's Jane and why is a small potato behind you?

Why didn't you just tell me this is what you were doing?

I don't know. My life is different than yours. You have your parents and your brother and your whole happy family. I just wanted to be somewhere else for a little while.

It's not like that. But whatever. You warned me you weren't looking for friends.

Unless they're virtual ones, I guess.

And the red team wins!

The next morning

YOU WERE ALREADY ASLEEP
WHEN I GOT IN. SORRY TO MISS
SEEING YOU. GO OUT AND GET
SOME FRESH AIR. I'LL KNO
IF YOU DON'T!
-DAD

Hey, I'm outside, aren't I?

Later
Professor Vargas told me Mateo has played the piano for years.
I didn't know that.

The next day
Well, I wanted an escape. May as well go halfway around the world.
WELCOME TO THE COLOSSEUM
I'm sure Mateo's seen this one a million times.
Wheeeee!!!
Faster, faster!
HISSSSS
ROAR

Did Run fall?
Nah, he left. Probably has a physical therapy appointment.
Oh! Did he get hurt or something?
Mom went to physical therapy after her accident. Or at least she *said* she went.
I thought you knew. He has permanent nerve damage in his legs so it's hard for him to walk or run.
10 POINTS!
I didn't realize. I'm sorry, I have to go.

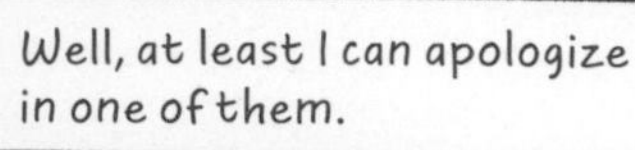

His Pay It Forward project for school?

He has a school project? I must miss more than I thought!

Beep
Beep
Huh?
NEW APPLICATION
GRAFFITI ROOM
IS NOW AVAILABLE
SOLO MODE IS ON
Almost me. Baby steps.
GRAFFITI ROOM

I go to school events for free food!

I LET THE PAST USE UP THE PRESENT

i believe in aliens

SOMETIMES I DONT TRUST MYSELF

i love her but she doesn't know i'm alive

I WISH I WAS

~~SHORTER~~

~~taller!!~~

~~smarter~~

~~CUTER~~

~~braver...~~

you're all perfect the way you are

That was intense.

Found Mateo's favorite spot, huh?

Is this seat taken?

What are you drawing?

I get not wanting to show anyone your work till it's done.
That's how I was with my VR game.

But when you're so close to something, you miss things other people spot. I added wearable weights after you suggested it in your survey.

It's a story my mom used to tell me about the world's longest living animal, a tortoise named Adwaitya.

You're really good. The turtle seems lonely, though. Maybe you can give him a friend.
Shay's so cute I'm not even going to correct him about the turtle.
Okay, yes I am.
Tortoise. And nothing I've read about his life said anything about friends.
Speaking of friends, Mateo's at the lab if you're looking for him.
How'd you know I was—
Snore

Hello?
Over here!
Where's everyone else? Other than Shay, who's napping under a tree.
They went to test out Lily's new portal.
Thanks. I'll go find them.
Or you could . . .
Sigh
Fine.

Empathy Project
Hey, doggies!
Oh no! Poor doggie!
SPRING HAVEN'S
LAST CHANCE PET ADOPTION

I didn't realize how much I missed my trips to the shelter.

Oh no, he can't get to his food!

Aw—they helped him!
JASPER

That feeling you're experiencing when you look at the injured dog? That's sympathy. Now watch it this way.
Wha? Am I a—

I'm a dog! I'm Jasper!

The other dogs are going to eat it all!

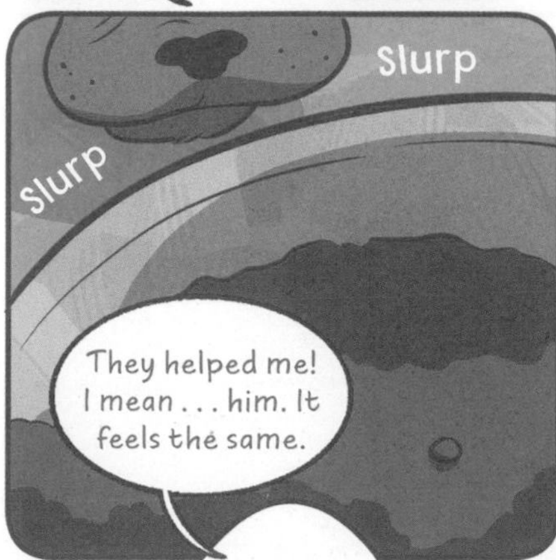
Slurp
Slurp
They helped me! I mean . . . him. It feels the same.

And that, my dear, is empathy.

Can't believe I'm going back for more.

It's your first day at a new school. How bad could it be?

What's that smell? Have you taken a shower in, like, a month?
Now that I think about it, it's been a few days.

She's totally going to fail this class!
Is she going to cry now?
They're not even giving me a chance.

Sort of like me with Mateo. I need to find him.
Right after I take a shower.

Even though they were NPCs, how powerful was that—from one to ten?

Ten!

Chapter Eight

ADDIE BRECKER...
GET READY FOR LIFTOFF
DESTINATION...
THE MOON

Fabric and wood from the Wright brothers' first attempt at flight, carried aboard the Apollo 11.
Your mission is to land your ship safely on the lunar surface so the moon seeds will actually have *touched* the moon this time!
Each seed you plant will reveal one *other* item that astronauts have brought into space.
Buzz Lightyear toy on the Discovery shuttle mission STS-124, bound for the International Space Station.
DS

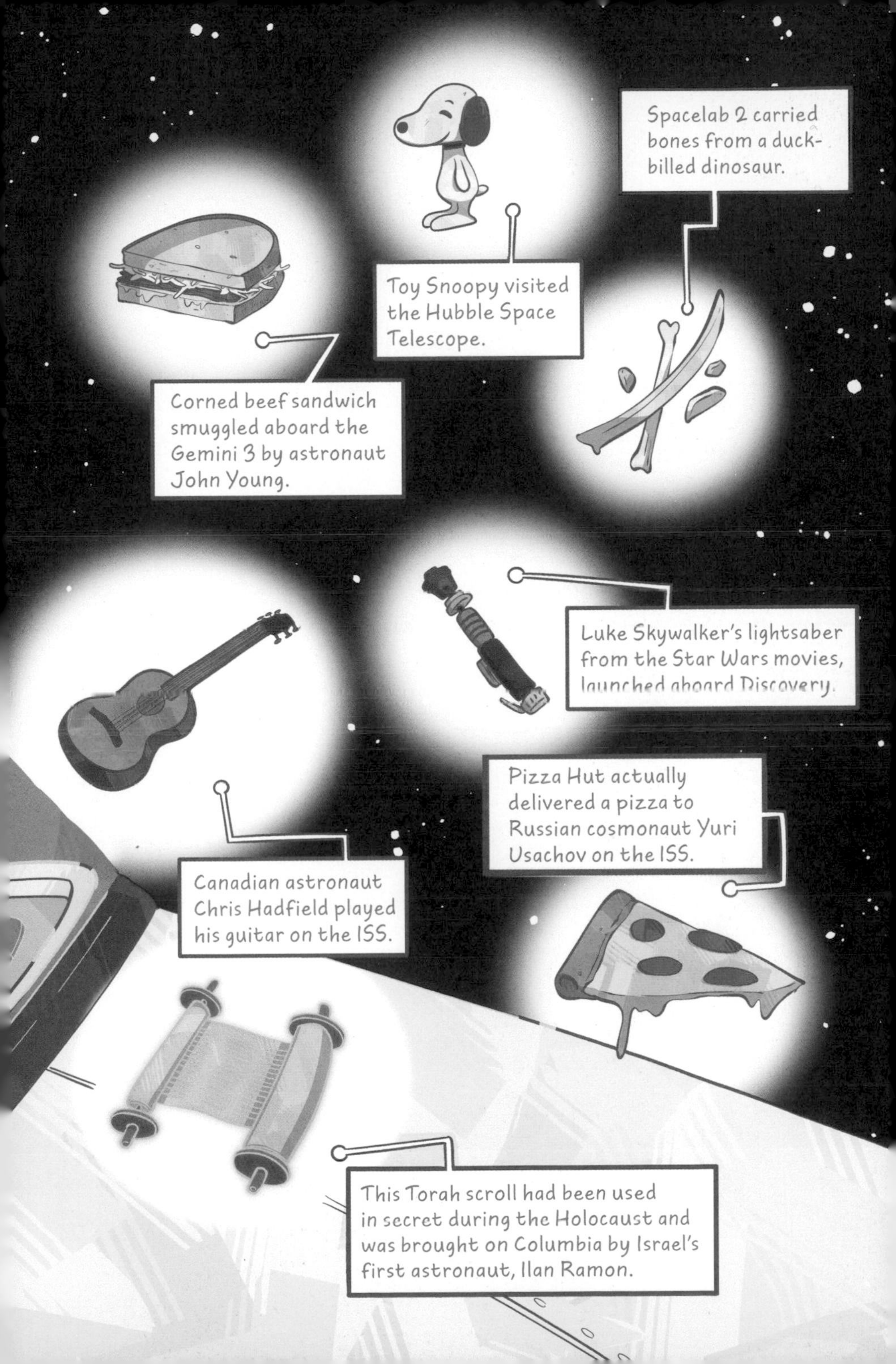
Toy Snoopy visited the Hubble Space Telescope.
Spacelab 2 carried bones from a duck-billed dinosaur.
Corned beef sandwich smuggled aboard the Gemini 3 by astronaut John Young.
Luke Skywalker's lightsaber from the Star Wars movies, launched aboard Discovery.
Pizza Hut actually delivered a pizza to Russian cosmonaut Yuri Usachov on the ISS.
Canadian astronaut Chris Hadfield played his guitar on the ISS.
This Torah scroll had been used in secret during the Holocaust and was brought on Columbia by Israel's first astronaut, Ilan Ramon.

Buzz
buzz

Hi, Dad, everything's fine.
Do you know where Mateo is?

Last I saw him he was headed for the hospital to do his volunteering.

Right. He does that. Because he's a good person.
Thanks, Dad.
And you'll be happy to know I did Surekha's demo.

I know.
She told you?
Nope.
Because you said "everything's fine" when you called so I wouldn't worry. That was very . . . *empathetic* of you.
Maybe there's hope for me yet.

I haven't been in a hospital since Dad and I brought Mom there.
C'mon, Addie. It's like the graffiti wall said. I've already let the past use up too much of the present.
Hi. I'm trying to find a volunteer named Mateo?
Take a visitor badge, head up to the second floor.

GET WELL SOON
6
5
4 Radiology
3 Orthopedic Clinic
2
1 Surgery Cardiology
L Main Lobby Pharmacy

we're gonna rock, rock, rock till—

NOAH
Honey, you only have three treatments left. I promise it won't hurt, and the hour will be over before you know it.
Pediatric Pathology & Infusion
Pediatric Pathology & Infusion
Community Room

Do you want to go in, Mr. Kowalsky? Take you back to your youth?
NURSE TRACY
Nothing can bring back my youth.
Hi. Are you a friend of our pianist?
I'm . . . not sure. I hope I still am.
For empathy you need to:
1. See from the other person's perspective.
2. Suspend judgment.
JUDGMENT
3. Be able to tap into your own feelings.
4. Communicate honestly so the other person feels heard and understood.
I want to go home!

Excuse me?

I, um, just wanted to say that even though I don't know exactly how you feel, I had to be in hospitals a lot, too, and I hated it.

You did?
Totally. Everyone tries to be nice, but it smells weird and no one wants to be here.

See, Mom? I'm not the only one!

Thank you.

If you want to hear Mateo play, his time is almost up.

I . . . I think I have to go.

MATEO'S SPOT

Support Group

Maybe I should have gone through that door.

I know my piano skills are outstanding, but I've never seen them bring someone to tears.

Thanks for coming.
Funny. You were good, though.
I've been trying to find you. I want to say I'm sorry for how I treated you. Your moon seeds demo was the best thing I've ever seen.
The Gang did most of the heavy lifting. I was hoping me and you could work on it together.
Let's do it!

My family has been through things, too. I would've understood wanting to escape. That's why I have my tree.
Our tree.

Our tree.

I heard from the nurse what you said to Noah. He finally agreed to get his chemo treatment.
I'm glad. I mean, not glad he has to get them, of course.
Do you play piano for the kids, too?
It doesn't have the same effect. I tried juggling once. Not a win.
Twenty minutes? It felt like five.
What if there is something that would make getting through their treatments easier?
When you're in VR, you're, like, fully there, and the real world fades away, right?
We can send the kids to the moon! Or to climb castles! They can watch movies or swim with dolphins or make 3D art or escape into a painting!
Such a great idea! I'm in!
You can escape into a painting?
It's gonna blow your mind.

A few days later
ADDIE AND MATEO'S CRASH COURSE ON CREATING VR
Latency: time between our head moving and the view updating
Tracking: how the VR device tracks the user's position and how they can move
Field of View (FOV): how wide an area you can see
Screen resolution and refresh rates: the number of pixels in rows/columns, and how many images are shown per second.
Haptics: the artificial sense of touch inside VR. Currently achieved by vibrations in a controller or wearables like gloves or vests

Mateo?
Sorry! Fascinating stuff, really. I'm sure you can fill me in.
Sigh.
I still need to explain how the software works, and it'll take at least two months to create content.
We have two weeks.
Ah, of course you do.
This will only take a few hours.
How to create VR CONTENT
Hold that thought. I've gotta go fetch a certain bike rider from the Great Wall of China.
PRIVATE MODE

Week One

2:37 PM
<Dr. Dave Williams>
To: <Addie Brecker>
From: <Addie Brecker>
Subject: Moon Trees in Virtual Reality
Dear Dr. Dave Williams at NASA,
My friend Mateo and I are making a virtual reality game where players bring seeds to the moon and back like Astronaut Roosa did. Can we have your permission to use your moon tree database? It would help us so much.
From, Addie Brecker, VR enthusiast, moon tree evangelist

And what if they could play with kids in other hospitals who—

Who are getting treatments at the same time!

We'll need to adjust the straps and interpupillary distance.
The what?

And I thought I was the one who didn't pay attention in VR class!

Got it! This will be perfect for the opening menu. Now we just need an on-camera announcer.

Count me in!

WE'RE IN A PAINTING!!

I like your new avatar. It's . . . better.
Thanks. Feels right.

I've never seen you work so hard on anything. You're making me very proud.
So here you'll point to your left and say, "Pull his claw to start the game."

Finally! I'm the queen of the castle!
Clap clap
Woo-hoo for Tortybutt!

Week Two
The Gang's first geocaching adventure!
Find the virtual geocache, get two power boosts. Then find some REAL caches hidden near some REAL moon trees!

I finally get to go inside one of Lily's portals!
Okay, that's wild!

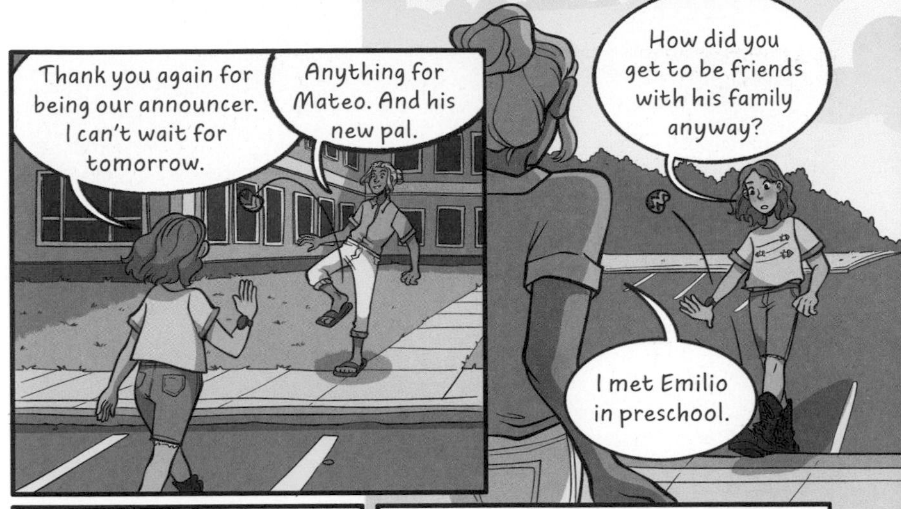
Thank you again for being our announcer. I can't wait for tomorrow.
Anything for Mateo. And his new pal.
How did you get to be friends with his family anyway?
I met Emilio in preschool.

Preschool?

My dad just called. We need to get permission slips from the head of the hospital or we can't start tomorrow. We've gotta hurry.

Guess I'm getting back on a bike.

SPRING HAVEN HOSPITAL

Dr. Jacobs? We were just on our way up to see you.
We're here to get the permission slips?

Your parents and the patients' parents need to sign before your project begins.

It protects the hospital if something goes wrong.

See to it that nothing goes wrong.

Friday morning
You look very nice. And this letter came for you.

You can just stick it in the desk drawer.
You'll want this one, I promise.
Rosemary *Roosa*? Roosa, like the astronaut who carried the moon seeds?
From the Desk of
Rosemary Roosa
r Addie,
good friend Dr. Dave Williams at
dard Space Flight Center forwarded yo
note. What a wonderful way for
e to learn about the moon trees!
d would be honored.

From the Desk of
Rosemary Roosa

Dear Addie,

My good friend Dr. Dave Williams at Goddard Space Flight Center forwarded your lovely note. What a wonderful way for people to learn about the moon trees! My dad would be honored. He always believed that as long as the moon trees have roots in the earth, the wonder of the moon missions will live on.

I would like to invite you and Mateo and your families to attend a special planting of a second-generation moon tree during the big solar eclipse next spring. I'll send the details as it gets closer.

All my best,
Rosemary

PS. If you want to be an astronaut, you can do it. Space needs more women!

Look what we got! Permission to use the moon tree database from the astronaut's daughter! Hey, your eyes look puffy.
I'm fine.
Morning, Mateo. Exciting day! Is your mom coming with us?
She had to go out of town. I promised a full report.
Okay, kids, get ready with your AR glasses when we pull up.
GO ADDIE AND MATEO
WE'RE SO PROUD OF YOU
LOVE THE GANG (AND DAD)
We're here, Dad! But you've gotta come down and see this!
Wait. What do you mean Noah's not coming?

Chapter Nine

I have pajamas like your shirt. I got mine at Kennedy Space Center. Is that where you got yours?
Her grandmother bought her the shirt. Cassidy loves outer space.
Right, honey?
Me too! How would you like to take a trip to the moon without leaving this chair? I think it might make getting your blood drawn much easier.
How?

I don't see anything.
Oh, wait! There's a menu and a cute surfer guy is talking to me!
Great! Now point at Moon Tree Rescue and press the trigger button.
I'm in space, Daddy! I'm really in space!
Ready?

Now everyone will know I've been here!

Okay, you can start now.

I'm already done.

Really? I didn't even feel it!

Can I have a turn?
Noah!

When it starts, aim the hose at the funny-looking monsters. And watch out for those sneaky kittens!
Ohhhh! Zombies are coming out!
HA HA HA HA!
Noah, I'm attaching this to your port.
Mom! Now I'm at a basketball game! A ball just swished over my head!
Free throw! And . . . he makes it in!
We should give them privacy.

I'd start playing, but I don't think that guy likes music, or maybe he just doesn't like me.
Don't take it personally. I heard him say that nothing could bring back his youth.
The map program!
Addresses to visit:
I'll try your toy, but I'm telling you, my childhood home, it's all gone. The Warsaw Ghetto, the uprising. Do they even teach it in schools?

If you want to
stop, just lift the
headset off.

Is it
working?

I'd have to
say yes.
Are you okay,
Mr. Kowalsky?
Do you want
to stop?
Gasp

It's still
there! I never
thought I'd
see it again!

Your old house?
Not the house. The *hill*. My sister Ryka and I used to roll down it.
That's where the corner bakery used to be.
And there's the pond where Poppa used to go ice fishing until he fell in and our grandmother put an end to that!
Are you okay? Should we stop?
If you don't mind, I'd like to sit on the hillside a little longer.
I haven't felt this close to my sister in eighty years.
I'll keep you company.

Guess what? My treatment is done! I played paintball with my new friend Austin!
He lives in Brazil. This was *his* third treatment, too!

We're going to meet again for the next one! I mean, I can, can't I?
Absolutely!

ZZZZZ

See you in two weeks!

I honestly don't know how to thank you for this.
You're the only reason he finally agreed to come today.

Later
ADDIE! How'd it go?
It was the *best*. We couldn't have done any of it without all of you.
That's so great! Where's Mateo?
He and his dad went for a walk. Where's Shay? I promised a little girl named Cassidy I'd tell him how cute he is.
He's not in today, but he left this for Mateo.
M— I think I found what you were looking for —S
It must be the location of the last moon trees we need for the game.

Mateo, are you home? I have your headset from Shay.
Knock knock
Guess I'm on my own for dinner.
Dad finally admitted he's too busy to cook every night.
the Dino King
How about we give Adwaitya a friend after all?

What animal has the shortest life span?

MAYFLY

Hmmm, what about the next shortest?
DRAGONFLY

A perfect pair.

I think I deserve a VR break.

ELM
PINE
This must be the location of one of the moon trees! Don't see a tree, though.

EMILIO VARGAS
What? No!
EMILIO VARGAS
OUR ANGEL
FOREVER IN OUR HE
JULY 18, 2
That's twenty years ago *today*! Why didn't I think it was weirder that he was never around? I never stepped on a single Lego.
This is why Shay said he and Emilio were friends in preschool, which made no sense.

And why Mateo's eyes were puffy this morning!

Let me guess. . . .
Cats knock you off the castle wall again?

I am so, so sorry, Mateo.

For what? Wasn't it amazing today? Put this one on. You have to see what Noah did.

But I need to tell you some—
This will just take a minute.

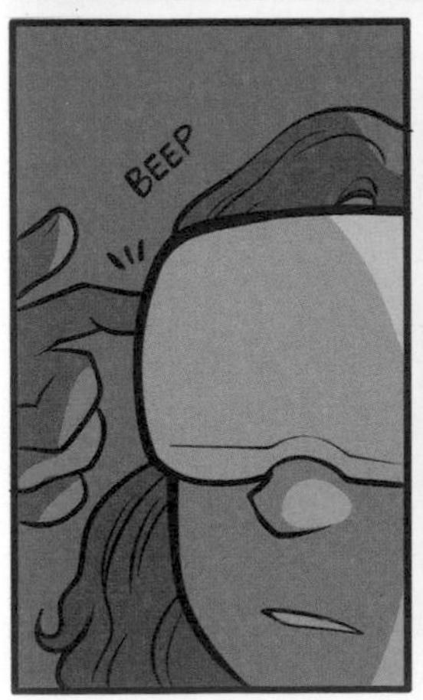
BEEP

SuperNoah
LET'S GET THIS
I BELIEVE IN YOU
Try the
See you next week
THX 4 EVERYTHING
YOU DID IT!!

Isn't it great? He's trying to help other kids. And he turned himself into a warrior!
It's so great . . . but, Mateo, listen . . .
And Mr. Kowalsky! My dad said he didn't stop talking about it all day, and he never talks to the other patients.
Mateo, listen— Shay said your bike program had found what you were looking for, and I thought I was going to see a tree but it wasn't a tree and I'm so, so sorry.
Oh.
Oh.

The accident happened before I was born.
And it's weird because even though I didn't know him, I still feel like I lost him.
My parents don't know that I've been trying to find that intersection for years.
There are 9,640 Park Roads and 8,232 Second Streets in the country. I'd pretty much given up, but Shay showed me a way to let the VR bike program search on its own.
I didn't know about the roadside memorial. That must e where my mom goes every year when she disappears for the day.
The Pay it Forward project isn't actually for school. It's the only thing I have of his.

I didn't tell you because I don't like people feeling sorry for me.

Trust me. I get that. I'm sorry that I said things that might've made you feel worse.
This isn't me feeling sorry for you. It's me apologizing.

I'll accept it. C'mon. I have one more thing for you to see. This is a happy one.

This tiny seed bravely traveled to the moon and back on Apollo 14 and is planted here on our nation's bicentennial.
"May this tree serve as a living symbol of our spectacular human and scientific achievements. May it inspire us to strive for the kind of growth that benefits our own citizens and all mankind."
—President Gerald Ford

I can't believe it! When did you find out?
I've always known. I was just waiting for the right moment to show you.
I'm too happy to be touching a real moon tree to be mad at you.

I have something big to tell you, too. It's about my mom.

Chapter Ten
A few weeks later
Woo-hoo!!
All right!!
YASSSS!
Wow, they're really happy to see us!
Pretty sure this isn't about us.
The Gang got their grants! Their projects are going to be out in the world!

Hurrah!
Taffy for everyone!
What are you guys going to do with *your* share of the money?
Our share?
I added your hospital project to my grant proposal. I got funded, so you got funded!!
We know *exactly* what to do with it!

VR headsets for everyone!

We hope you like the special area we made for you.
ADDIE & MATEO'S VIRTUAL REALITY CORNER
CONTROLLERS
HEADSETS

It's beautiful.

This one is for you to keep. It's to celebrate your final treatment.
We'll see you in VR, right?

Hooray!!

See, Shelly? I told you we'd be going home.

Ding dong

One for the road?
I'm gonna miss these.

Why don't you ever want to come in?

This used to be where my parents lived with Emilio.

Huh. It looks just like the other apartments in the building.
This room would have been my parents' . . . and your room would have been his.
Nice tortoise.
It's a—oh, you actually got it right.

Of course. Turtles and tortoises look totally different.

I guess I always pictured that his room would be the same as he left it. Isn't that weird? So many other people have stayed here over the years.
Wait, there might actually be something from him.
Maybe. It's nice to think so.
This is for you and your dad to remember us by when you're back in the big city.
Taffy from the candy factory?
The third one's for your mom.

See you in VR!
Bye!
Safe travels!
Bon voyage!

Chapter Eleven

After that concert I put away my clarinet for good.

Let me get you the help you need.
I just need to sleep.
OPIOD
OW
E SIGNS
One in three people prescribed painkillers for injury will become addicted in a month
I didn't really know what was going on. Or maybe I just didn't want to see it.
But soon I had no choice.

DATE
PATIENT
DOCTOR
Rx
PRESCRIPTION
Faking the prescription was bad enough.
Selling some of the pills was even worse.

And that's when she got caught.
I'm so, so sorry.
I didn't care if she was sorry. Or that she was going somewhere to get healthy and serve her sentence. All I knew was that she'd left me.

I think it's harder to have empathy for the people we love the most.
When they do something wrong it feels so personal.
But I have to do this.
For her, and also for me.
Hi, Mom.
VISITOR

Lightning! This is where he'd been all this time.

It took a little time, but slowly we found our way back to each other.
TORTYBUTT
LIGHTNINGMOM
And Mom got to go to the moon after all . . . virtually.

VR Dance Party
Dad got the whole gang these body trackers that haven't even come out yet.

Mateo prefers swimming to dancing.
Mom's early wish for me came true. I see wonder everywhere now. I'd just forgotten to look for it.

Chapter Twelve

I finally get to meet Jasper the dog in real life!
Surekha was so excited when the Vargas family adopted him. But not as excited as Mateo!

Hello, Mateo. It's lovely meeting you.

My hair's not usually blue. I found a box from last summer. Long story.
I like it.

Me too.

Brought you something.
ONE DAY AND FOREVER:
THE ALMOST TRUE STORY
OF THE REAL LIFE TORTOISE ADWAITYA
TO MATEO, MY INSPIRATION FOR ADWAITYA'S FRIENDSHIP WITH SAMEER, A DRAGONFLY. LIKE US, THEIR TIME TOGETHER WAS SHORT, BUT YOU MADE A BIG DIFFERENCE IN ALL THE OTHER DAYS TO COME.
Totality! Glasses off!
Ohhhh!
Ahhh!

Don't forget
to look up!

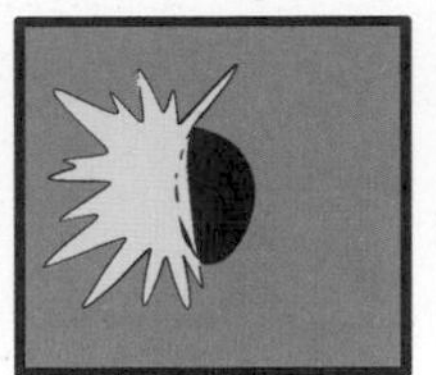

Ready to go meet the astronaut's daughter?
Don't Look Back You're Not Going That Way

One day when you go into space, I'll be called "the astronaut's mom."

It's been a long road, but we've learned how to be a family again.

Actually, Mom, things are pretty great on the ground.

Don't Look Back You're Not Going That Way

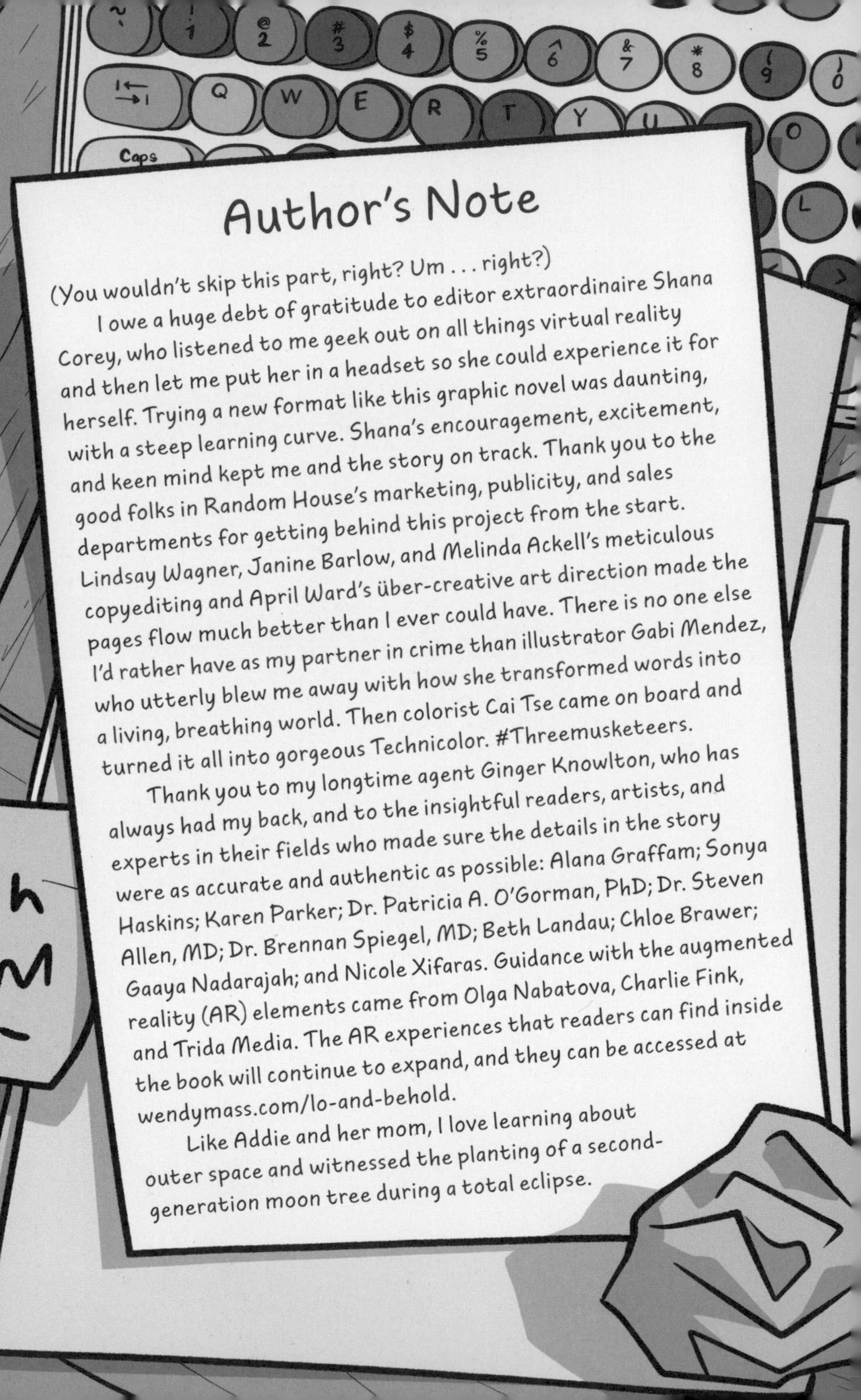

Author's Note

(You wouldn't skip this part, right? Um . . . right?)

I owe a huge debt of gratitude to editor extraordinaire Shana Corey, who listened to me geek out on all things virtual reality and then let me put her in a headset so she could experience it for herself. Trying a new format like this graphic novel was daunting, with a steep learning curve. Shana's encouragement, excitement, and keen mind kept me and the story on track. Thank you to the good folks in Random House's marketing, publicity, and sales departments for getting behind this project from the start. Lindsay Wagner, Janine Barlow, and Melinda Ackell's meticulous copyediting and April Ward's über-creative art direction made the pages flow much better than I ever could have. There is no one else I'd rather have as my partner in crime than illustrator Gabi Mendez, who utterly blew me away with how she transformed words into a living, breathing world. Then colorist Cai Tse came on board and turned it all into gorgeous Technicolor. #Threemusketeers.

Thank you to my longtime agent Ginger Knowlton, who has always had my back, and to the insightful readers, artists, and experts in their fields who made sure the details in the story were as accurate and authentic as possible: Alana Graffam; Sonya Haskins; Karen Parker; Dr. Patricia A. O'Gorman, PhD; Dr. Steven Allen, MD; Dr. Brennan Spiegel, MD; Beth Landau; Chloe Brawer; Gaaya Nadarajah; and Nicole Xifaras. Guidance with the augmented reality (AR) elements came from Olga Nabatova, Charlie Fink, and Trida Media. The AR experiences that readers can find inside the book will continue to expand, and they can be accessed at wendymass.com/lo-and-behold.

Like Addie and her mom, I love learning about outer space and witnessed the planting of a second-generation moon tree during a total eclipse.

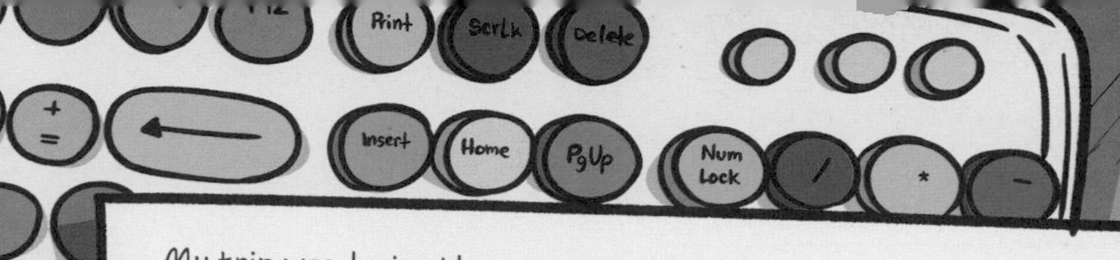

My trip was during the summer of 2017, on a mountaintop in North Carolina. I was lucky enough to meet Rosemary Roosa there and to hear the story of her dad's moon seeds. I am honored that she and Dr. Dave Williams (who really does maintain a listing of moon trees for NASA) agreed to be characters in this book.

Growing up, I earned the nickname Gadget Girl because I loved gadgets and the latest technology. If you could buy it from Radio Shack (I miss that place!) or the back of a comic book, I spent my babysitting money on it. The pages that follow will show you how these early interests led to me standing in the summer heat to purchase the first commercially available VR headset the day it came out. (I could have just waited for it to arrive in the mail the next day but seriously, c'mon!)

If you're excited to experience virtual reality for yourself (and I hope you are), check out the resources section of my website: wendymass.com. You'll find discussions of my favorite VR games and apps, comparisons of different headsets, and information on using the technology with seniors, for community-building, and in areas like education and healthcare. There is a section dedicated to creating your own AR, VR, and 360-degree content. You can even discover Mateo's geocaching tips, information on all things moon tree, and hopefully one day even a copy of Addie's picture book!

You will also find further reading and guidance on the more serious themes from the book, like empathy, loss, and addiction. If you or someone you know is struggling, please understand that you are not alone and you don't have to go through it alone. It can be hard not to blame yourself or to feel betrayed if someone you love is pulling away, but resentment hurts you far more than the other person and compassion is always free. Remember to save some for yourself.

The phrase "lo and behold" is used to express wonder or surprise. Wear wonder like a cape. It will help sustain and strengthen you as you ride the always-surprising roller coaster of life.

See you in VR. Wendy Mass

A Short History of Gadget Girl

(That's Me, Wendy)

Hi, I'm Wendy. I've always loved technology. As a kid, peering into this old-timey movie projector at our local shoe store made me feel like I was being transported somewhere else.

My neighbor got the first home video game, and I played for hours. I can still hear that little bleep sound as the "ball" hit the "paddle."

When I turned thirteen, my parents gave me a ring. It made me feel very grown-up. In the sunlight, the stone turned from green to purple.

Until one day it did more than that! It was a solid ten minutes before I realized the ring was reflecting the view outside my classroom window and not a magical portal to a parallel universe.

Holograms and 3D images captivated me. I loved the idea that something was there and not there, depending on how you looked at it.
The '90s were a fun time for Gadget Girl.
You can draw something on a piece of paper and feed it into a machine in one place, and it comes out in another place! The *same drawing*!
As one of the first ten people in the world with a DVR, I was an "early adopter" before that was a thing.
You can *pause* live TV?? Are you a *time wizard*??

Lucid dreaming camp is a real thing! The mask blinks while you're in REM sleep to help you recognize you're dreaming.

Sure, my friends bolted when I pulled out the metal detector, but I found enough quarters to buy funnel cake and a caramel apple. So who had the last laugh?

And today if the internet doesn't connect within two milliseconds, it feels like an eternity. I love all the methods we have to connect with each other and to get information.

But virtual reality, man. This just blew my mind. It felt like everything else had only been leading up to it. Slipping on that first headset was like stepping into a lucid dream, but one you didn't have to be asleep to experience. I set a goal for myself to find something new in VR each day that would make my jaw drop. I haven't run out yet.
Like Addie, I am moved to tears with the ways medical facilities are using VR to distract patients from their pain and to help them heal faster with the need for less medication.
Nursing homes are sparking their residents' memories by taking them on virtual trips around the world. This technology fosters empathy, brings people together, educates, entertains, and inspires creativity and wonder.
And we could all use more of that.

Hi, this is Gabi, the artist for *Lo and Behold*!! Like a lot of artists, I've been drawing all my life and reading comics for just as long. I read a loooot of manga growing up and jumped right into indie comics as a teen, so don't ask me anything about superheroes! Chica Umino and Faith Erin Hicks, though? We can talk. I love making and reading comics about friendship and finding the things in life that make you feel like you belong.
I was really excited to delve into Addie's world and to bring her to life in a way that worked for how Wendy and I both pictured her.
Silly and sweet
And a little mischievous
Mateo
smaller eyes will also make her read a little older
A little less Elliot Page/ 90's grunge
SPACE CASE
Trying not to laugh at Dad's pun
The whole gang went through a few changes until everyone was book-ready! Luckily there was plenty of time for some back and forth, as you can see on the next page...

The book was finished in five stages: thumbnail sketches, tight pencil lines, inked lines, color (by the fantastic Cai Tse!), and then text boxes on top. The thumb stage is very loose, just to get an idea of how the page will look laid out. The next two stages are full of tweaking and refining, and then color brings it all to life! Comics are a team sport for sure. Me and Wendy and the editorial team got to bounce ideas off each other for the whole process!
I hope you enjoyed reading *Lo and Behold* as much as I enjoyed drawing it! Be the dragonfly to the tortoises in your life, don't be afraid to try new things, and I hope to see you in my next comic!
SID!!

Wendy Mass is the *New York Times* bestselling author of thirty books for young readers (which have been translated into twenty-six languages and nominated for ninety-one state awards), including the Schneider Family Book Award winner *A Mango-Shaped Space*, the bestselling Willow Falls and Candymakers series, *Jeremy Fink and the Meaning of Life* (which was made into a feature film), and *Bob* (coauthored with Rebecca Stead). Wendy's hobbies include geocaching, virtual reality, and learning magic tricks. *Lo and Behold* is her graphic novel debut. She lives with her family in New Jersey and online at wendymass.com and on Instagram at wendy_mass.

Gabi Mendez is a queer Latinx comics artist and illustrator and is making her graphic novel debut with *Lo and Behold*. Originally from San Pedro, California, Gabi is a graduate of the School of the Art Institute of Chicago and the sequential art master's program at SCAD. She writes a lot of silly comics, says "dude" too much, and just wants everyone to feel included. Gabi lives in Chicago, where she's working on her next middle-grade graphic novel. You can visit her online at gabimendez.com and @hobbleshmobble.

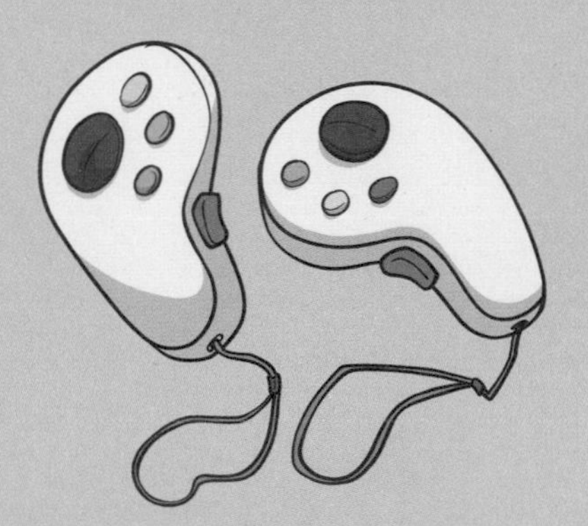

If you change the way you look at things,
the things you look at change.

–Dr. Wayne Dyer